This Book belongs to:

marley wittkap

igloo

Published in 2012
by Igloo Books Ltd
Cottage Farm,
Sywell,
NN6 0BJ
www.igloo-books.com

10 9 8

ISBN: 978 0 85734 149 5

Project Managed by Page to Page
Designed by Chris Fraser

Printed and manufactured in China

Fairytales
for Girls

Retold by Nick Ellsworth

Illustrated by Stephen Aitken • Sahin Erkocak

Marcy Ramsey • Gary Rees • Elena Selivanova

Contents

For Younger Children

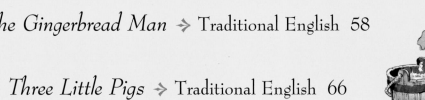

For Older Children

Goldilocks and The Three Bears

Once upon a time there was a lovely little cottage that sat right in the middle of the woods. In this cottage lived a family of friendly bears. There was Big Papa Bear, who could be a little grumpy at times, Medium-sized Mama Bear, who was just as a mother should be and Teenie Weenie Baby Bear, who liked to play all day.

One fine day they all stomped down to the kitchen for their usual breakfast of delicious homemade porridge. Papa Bear ate his porridge out of a big bowl, Mama Bear ate her porridge out of a medium-sized bowl, while Teenie Weenie Baby Bear had his very own teenie weenie bowl.

Papa Bear scooped up a large spoonful of porridge and popped it straight into his mouth. "Ouch," he cried. "That's too hot!" Mama Bear tasted hers. "Ooh, I suppose it is a bit hot," she agreed.
"It will burn my mouth!" cried Teenie Weenie Baby Bear after tasting his.

"I've got a good idea," said Mama Bear. "Why don't we go for a walk in the woods? By the time we get back, our porridge will be cool."
"Oh, all right," said Papa Bear a bit grumpily. He really would have liked to go back to bed until his porridge cooled down.
"Yippee!" yelled Teenie Weenie Baby Bear. "I can show you how fast I can run."
So, shutting the door behind them, the three bears went for a walk in the woods.

Not long after they had gone, a little girl called Goldilocks, who was out walking in the woods, stumbled across the little cottage where the three bears lived. She thought it was so lovely that she wanted to look inside. She carefully opened the door and shut it quietly behind her.

The first thing she noticed were the three bowls of porridge on the kitchen table.

"They look really yummy," she thought. "I'm so hungry. I'm sure no one would mind if I ate just a little."

First, she tried a spoonful of porridge from the big bowl. But that was too salty.

Next, she tried a spoonful of porridge from the medium-sized bowl. But that was too sweet.

Finally, she tried a spoonful of porridge from the teenie weenie bowl. That was just right. Goldilocks was so hungry she ate every last bit. She felt tired after eating so much and decided to sit down for a while.

First, she tried to sit in a big chair but it was so big, her feet didn't even touch the ground.

Next, she tried a medium-sized chair. That was a little better but she could only reach the ground with her toes.

Finally, she sat in a teenie weenie chair and that was just right. But she was far too big for the teenie weenie chair and, when she sat down in it, she broke it!

"I wonder if there are any beds upstairs," she thought. "I'm sure no one would mind if I lay down for a while."

She went upstairs and saw three beds.

The first bed she tried was a big, floppy bed. "This bed is far too soft," she thought.

The next bed was a very neat, medium-sized bed. "This bed is far too hard," she thought.

Finally, she lay on a teenie weenie bed. "This bed is just right," thought Goldilocks, and was soon fast asleep.

When the three bears returned from their walk, they were very hungry and looking forward to eating their porridge. The first thing they saw were the spoons lying in the porridge bowls.

"Who's been eating my porridge?" cried Papa Bear in a big, grumpy voice.

"Who's been eating my porridge?" cried Mama Bear in a medium-sized voice.

"Who's been eating my porridge, and eaten it all up?" cried Teenie Weenie Baby Bear in a teenie weenie voice.

Papa Bear was so grumpy he decided to have a sit down, but noticed that the cushion on his chair was messed up.

"Who's been sitting in my chair?" he cried in his big, grumpy voice.

"Who's been sitting in my chair?" cried Mama Bear in her medium-sized voice, noticing that her cushion was messed up, too.

"And who's been sitting in my chair and broken it?" yelled Teenie Weenie Baby Bear in his teenie weenie voice.

"This is making me really grumpy," said Papa Bear in his big, grumpy voice. "I'm going to bed." The other bears agreed and followed him up the stairs.

When they got there, they saw that their beds had been messed up, too.

"Who's been sleeping in my bed?" cried Papa Bear in his big, grumpy voice.

"Who's been sleeping in my bed?" cried Mama Bear in her medium-sized voice.

"And who's been sleeping in my bed, and is still sleeping in my bed?" cried Teenie Weenie Baby Bear in his teenie weenie voice.

14

All this shouting woke Goldilocks. When she saw the three bears looking down angrily at her, she leaped out of bed, ran down the stairs, out the door and into the woods as fast as she could. And the three bears were very pleased that they never saw her, ever again.

Jack and The Beanstalk

Jack lived with his mother in an old cottage in a field. They were very poor. The only thing they owned was a cow called Milky-white. One day, poor old Milky-white stopped giving them milk. "You'd better take her to the market and sell her," Jack's mother told him. "At least we'll be able to buy some bread and honey with the money we get for her."

The next morning, Jack and Milky-white set out bright and early on the road to the market. Halfway there, Jack noticed an old man sitting at the side of the road.

"Fine morning," said Jack.

"It certainly is," said the man. "What a fine looking cow you have there."

"I'm taking her to the market to sell her," replied Jack.

"Perhaps you would sell her to me," said the old man. "I have no money, but I do have five magic beans I could give you."

Jack thought this was a very fair exchange. After saying goodbye to Milky-white, he put the magic beans safely in his pocket and ran home to his mother. When he'd told her what had happened and showed her the magic beans, she was furious with him.

"You stupid boy," she said. "You may as well have given our cow away. Now, we have nothing to eat and no money to buy any food. Go to your room at once!"

Then she threw the beans out the window.

When Jack woke up the next morning, there was a strange shadow over his bed. He looked out the window and couldn't believe his eyes. Overnight, one of the beans had grown into a huge beanstalk. It was so big, he couldn't see the top. It just disappeared into the clouds.

Jack stepped out his window onto the beanstalk and started to climb. He went higher and higher until he couldn't see the ground at all. At the very top, was a rough track. He followed the track until he came to a huge castle. He walked around the castle walls until he came to a great door. He crept inside and found himself inside an immense kitchen.

Suddenly, he came face to face with an enormous woman.
"Ah, a little boy," she said. "My husband loves to eat little boys for breakfast. Lucky for you, I've already made him breakfast today."
Suddenly, Jack heard footsteps. They were so loud, they shook the whole castle.
"Quick, hide!" said the enormous woman.

"That's my husband coming. He'll want to eat you if he sees you."
Jack hid among the gigantic pots and pans and saw a great big giant enter the kitchen. He sang a strange song in a big, rumbling voice.

"Fee, fi, fo, fum.
I smell the blood of an Englishman.
Be he alive or be he dead,
I'll grind his bones to make my bed."
Jack had never been so frightened in his life. He kept as still as possible.

Hiding behind the pots and pans, he watched as the giant sat down at a vast table and ate a huge breakfast of eggs, bacon and toast. After he'd finished eating, he pulled a bag of gold coins from his pocket and began to count them. The giant got halfway through counting the coins, before he leaned back in his chair and fell fast asleep. His snoring sounded like the rumble of thunder.

Jack carefully slipped out from his hiding place, tucked two of the huge gold coins under his arm, and quickly ran out of the castle and back to the beanstalk. He threw the coins down to his garden and climbed down as fast as he could.

When he reached the bottom, he found his mother staring in amazement

at the gold coins. When Jack told her his astonishing story, his mother couldn't help but believe him. The proof was right there in front of her: the two gold coins.

For the next few months, Jack and his mother had everything they wanted. They bought all the food they could eat and furnished their cottage from top to bottom. But, soon, the money ran out and Jack realized that he'd have to get more. So, up the beanstalk he went again. When he got to the kitchen this time, he hid in the massive oven. Just in time, because the ground began to shake as the giant stomped in for breakfast.

"Fee, fi, fo, fum.
I smell the blood of an Englishman.
Be he alive or be he dead,
I'll grind his bones to make my bed."

The giant sat down with a great thump and, like the last time, was served an enormous breakfast by his enormous wife. After he'd finished, he put a hen on the table.
"Oh, no. He's not going to eat that, too," thought Jack from his hiding place.
But the giant didn't eat it. He just roared, "Lay!" to the hen, and the hen laid a golden egg!
A few minutes later, the giant roared "Lay!" to the hen again. It laid another golden egg!
"I must have that hen," thought Jack. When the giant was sleeping, he sneaked out of the oven, grabbed the hen and ran as fast as he could to the beanstalk.
At the bottom, Jack's mother was astonished when she saw the hen

laying golden eggs, and gave Jack a great big hug. Jack became very rich. But he soon got bored having nothing to do, so he climbed the beanstalk once again.

When he reached the castle this time, he hid in the log basket. As usual,

the giant ate his huge breakfast. When he'd finished, he put a little harp on the table.

"Play!" roared the giant. The harp began to play the most beautiful music.

"I must have that harp," thought Jack. After the giant had fallen asleep, Jack climbed out of the log basket, snatched the harp from the table and ran out of the castle.

But the harp cried, "Help me, master! Help me, master!"

The giant woke with a start and, when he realized what was happening, chased Jack all the way to the beanstalk. Jack threw the harp down, and then began to climb down himself. Looking up, he saw that the giant was climbing down after him! The beanstalk was shaking and waving around under the giant's huge weight.

When Jack got to the bottom, he grabbed an axe and quickly chopped down the beanstalk. The giant came crashing to the ground and was killed at once.

There were no more adventures for Jack and his beanstalk. The harp

was broken but Jack and his mother still had the hen that laid golden eggs, so they never had to worry about anything ever again, and lived happily ever after.

Little Red Riding Hood

nce upon a time there was a nice little girl who lived with her mother in a nice little cottage at the edge of a deep, dark forest. The girl was known as Little Red Riding Hood because she always wore a beautiful red cape with a hood.

One day, her mother called to her from the kitchen. "Little Red Riding Hood, Granny is not feeling very well. Will you take her some goodies I've packed for her?"
"Of course I will," said Little Red Riding Hood, who loved her Granny very much.

She ran downstairs and peeked into the basket her mother had packed. It was full of delicious things. There were homemade cookies, a jam tart, some cherry muffins and, to finish it all off, the biggest, reddest apple that Little Red Riding Hood had ever seen.

Granny's cottage lay on the other side of the forest. "Now, remember," said Little Red Riding Hood's mother, "keep to the path and don't talk to any strangers."
"I won't," replied Little Red Riding Hood and, picking up the basket, she skipped merrily out the door.

It was a lovely day and Little Red Riding Hood sang a merry tune to herself as she made her way along the path.

A little while later, when she was in the deepest, darkest part of the forest, she saw some pretty flowers growing in a small clearing just off the path. "I'm sure Mother wouldn't mind if I went off the path for a minute to pick some flowers. Granny would love them," she thought. She had a quick look around, didn't see anyone, so ran to the little clearing, where she started to pick the flowers.

But, hiding behind a tree, was a not-very-nice wolf, who was hungry and looking for his dinner. In one swift movement, he was at Little Red Riding Hood's side.

"Hello, my dear," he said, in his most charming voice. "What a beautiful day! I see you're picking flowers. May I help you?"

Little Red Riding Hood was startled to see the wolf at first, but he seemed so friendly and had such a lovely deep voice, her fears faded away. "I'm picking them for my Granny. She's not very well. I'm taking her this basket of food."

"What a lovely thing to do!" exclaimed the wolf, thinking that if he was clever, he might be able to eat the girl, her Granny and the basket of food for his dinner.

"I've got an idea," said the wolf. "Why don't I run ahead and give the basket to your Granny, while you finish picking your pretty flowers. Then we can all meet at her house. Hmm?"

"That's a very good idea," said Little Red Hiding Hood. "She lives a little further up the path in the first cottage."

"That's settled, then," said the wolf, taking the basket from her. "By the way, what's your name?"

"Little Red Riding Hood," she answered.

"Charmed to meet you, my dear," said the wolf, with a big, wide grin. "See you soon."

And he set off down the path towards Granny's cottage, licking his lips.

When he arrived at Granny's cottage, he knocked on the door.
"Hello! Is there anyone at home?" shouted the wolf in his best little
girl's voice.
"Who's there?" asked Granny, tucked up in bed.
"It's me, Granny," said the wolf, "Little Red Riding Hood."
"Come in, dear," said Granny. "I'm in bed."

The wolf opened the door and ran upstairs, into Granny's bedroom.
"You're not Little Red Riding Hood!" exclaimed Granny.
"You're absolutely right!" said the wolf, and before she had a chance
to say anything else, he leapt over to her bedside, opened his mouth as
wide as he could, and gobbled Granny right up.
"And now for Little Red Riding Hood," thought the wolf. He put on
Granny's shawl, nightcap and glasses as fast as he could, and dived into
the bed.
"What a clever wolf I am," he chuckled to himself.

A short time later, Little Red Riding Hood arrived at Granny's cottage and knocked on the door.

"Who's there?" asked the wolf in his best Granny voice.

"It's me, Granny. Little Red Riding Hood," said Little Red Riding Hood.

"Let yourself in, dear," said the wolf.

Little Red Riding Hood opened the door and went into Granny's bedroom.

"What big eyes you have," said Little Red Riding Hood.

"All the better to see you with, my dear," replied the wolf.

"What big ears you have," said Little Red Riding Hood.

"All the better to hear you with, my dear," replied the wolf.

"And what big teeth you have," said Little Red Riding Hood.

"All the better to EAT you with!" said the wolf, and leaped out of bed and gobbled her up in an instant. Still feeling hungry, the wolf also ate all the food in the basket. Then he gave a huge burp.

But, a woodcutter working nearby had heard all the noise coming from Granny's cottage. He burst through the door and, when he saw the wolf, killed him with one mighty blow of his axe. Then he slit open the wolf's tummy and Little Red Riding Hood and her Granny popped out, alive and well. They were so relieved to be rescued, they hugged each other tightly.

"Thank you!" said Granny to the woodcutter.

"I'm only happy that you and Little Red Riding Hood are safe," he replied.

"I hope this teaches you never to talk to strangers again," said Granny to Little Red Riding Hood.

Little Red Riding Hood promised that she wouldn't, and she never did, however charming and helpful they seemed to be.

Snow White

 ne winter's day, a Queen sat at a window, sewing. Suddenly, she pricked her finger and a drop of blood fell onto the snow below. She liked the bright red of the blood against the whiteness of the snow. She hoped that one day she would give birth to a child with lovely, snow-white skin and bright, blood-red lips.

The very next year, the Queen gave birth to a baby daughter. The baby had the whitest of skin and the reddest of lips. The Queen called her child Snow White and she loved her daughter dearly. Sadly, the Queen died the very same year.

After some time, Snow White's father, the King, married again. His new Queen was very beautiful but she was also vain and proud. She owned a special mirror, and every morning she asked the mirror the same question.

"Mirror, mirror, on the wall, who is the fairest of them all?"

"You are, O Queen," the mirror would also reply.

And every morning the Queen would smile to herself, for she knew that the mirror always told the truth.

As the years passed, Snow White was slowly turning into a beautiful young woman. One morning, the Queen awoke and asked the mirror her usual question.

"Mirror, mirror, on the wall, who is the fairest of them all?"

But this time, the mirror replied:

"You, O Queen, are fair, it's true, but Snow White is now fairer than you."

The Queen turned green with envy. No one was allowed to be more beautiful than her. Even though Snow White was dearly loved by the King, the twisted, jealous Queen decided to have her killed as soon as possible. She summoned the royal huntsman and told him to take Snow White into the forest and kill her. She told him to cut out Snow White's

heart and bring it to her, to prove that she was dead.

The huntsman took Snow White into the forest, but, as he was about to kill her, looked at her frightened face. He felt so sorry for her, he told her to run away and hide deeper in the forest. Then he killed a wild boar and cut out its heart so he could pretend that it was Snow White's heart, when he showed it to the Queen.

Snow White ran further and further into the forest. When she could run no more, she stopped and leaned against a tree to get her breath back. Out of the corner of her eye she noticed a small cottage, half hidden by the trees. She went up to the cottage and knocked on the door. There

was no reply. She opened the door and went in.

In front of her was a little table with seven little cups and seven little plates on it. There was food on the plates and water in the cups. The cottage belonged to seven dwarfs who worked all day in a silver mine. Snow White was very hungry and thirsty, so she took a little bit of food from each plate, and a little bit of water from each cup. She was a very thoughtful girl and didn't want to empty one person's plate and cup completely. After she'd eaten, she felt very tired. She went upstairs and found a room with seven beds in it. She lay down on one of the beds

and fell fast asleep.

When the seven dwarfs returned home, they each found a little bit of food missing from their plates and a little bit of water missing from their cups. When they went upstairs, they found something even stranger. There was a beautiful young girl sleeping in one of their beds! They woke her and asked her what she was doing there. Snow White burst into tears and, after she'd stopped crying, told them her terrible story. The seven dwarfs felt so sorry for her, they invited her to stay with them. "But I can't pay you anything for my food and bed," Snow White cried. "I have no money."

The dwarfs told her, that as long as she cooked and kept the cottage clean for them, she was welcome to stay as long as she liked.

"Thank you so much. I'll do my best to look after you," said Snow White, happily.

Back at the castle, the wicked Queen took what she thought was Snow White's heart and had great pleasure feeding it to the dogs. The next morning, she stood in front of her mirror.

"Mirror, mirror, on the wall, who is the fairest of them all?"

"You, O Queen, are fair, it's true, but Snow White is still fairer than you," the mirror replied.

The Queen screamed in anger. She knew that the mirror never lied, so Snow White must still be alive. She found out where Snow White was living and decided to play a horrible trick on her. The Queen disguised herself as a peddler selling little trinkets, pieces of lace and pretty brooches, and went to the dwarfs' cottage and knocked on the door.

"Hello, my dear," croaked the Queen, pretending to be the peddler. "I've got some lovely little things here you may care to see."

"Oh, isn't it lovely!" Snow White exclaimed, as the Queen held up a pretty bow.

The Queen convinced Snow White that she needed a new length of braid for her bodice but, when she helped Snow White put it on, she pulled it so tightly that all the breath went out of Snow White's body. The Queen left her, believing she was dead.

When the seven dwarfs arrived home from work that evening, they were shocked to find Snow White lying on the floor. She didn't seem to be breathing. When they saw how tightly her bodice was tied, they quickly cut it loose. The dwarfs were relieved and delighted when she started to breathe again. They made her promise them that she'd never accept anything from a stranger in future.

Meanwhile, the Queen rushed back to the palace, ripped off her disguise and stood in front of her mirror.

"Mirror, mirror, on the wall, who is the fairest of them all?" she asked.
"You, O Queen, are fair, it's true, but Snow White is still fairer than
you," the mirror replied.

The Queen was speechless with rage when she realised that Snow
White was still alive.

"I'll think of another way to trick her," she thought. "And this time,
death will not escape her!"

The Queen picked an apple that had one red side and one yellow side.
She then injected a deadly poison into the red side and disguised herself
once more: this time as an old peasant woman. She went to the dwarfs'
cottage and knocked on the door again. Snow White went to answer
the knock, and was a little wary at first, but the old peasant woman was
so nice and friendly, she quickly relaxed and they were soon chatting

away.

After they had been talking for some time, the disguised Queen offered Snow White the poisoned apple.

"That's very kind of you," said Snow White. "But I'm not supposed to take anything from strangers."

"Don't worry. There's nothing wrong with this apple," said the Queen. "And to prove it to you, I'll take a bite out of it first."

With a great crunch, the Queen took a large bite out of the yellow side of the apple. Then she offered the poisoned, red side to Snow White.

"I suppose it's all right, and it does look delicious," said Snow White. As soon as she had taken a bite out of the apple, the poor girl fell dead at the Queen's feet. The Queen rushed back to the palace and ripped off her disguise.

"Mirror, mirror, on the wall, who is the fairest of them all?" she asked the mirror.

"You are, O Queen," it replied.

The Queen shrieked with joy. She had succeeded. Snow White was well and truly dead.

When the dwarfs arrived home that evening, they could not wake Snow White. They stayed with her all night, hoping that she might wake up, but in the morning they realized that she must be dead. With heavy hearts, they put her on a bed and, with bowed heads, stood guard over her. Snow White remained beautiful, even in death.

Years passed, and news of Snow White's beauty had spread far and wide. One day, a Prince decided to see the beautiful girl for himself. Her beauty took his breath away and he fell in love with her instantly. Tenderly, the Prince lifted Snow White's head to kiss her. But as he did so, the tiny piece of apple that had poisoned her, fell from her lips. Gradually, she began to stir.

"What has happened?" she asked drowsily.

The seven dwarfs jumped up and down with joy that she was alive.

When Snow White's father, the King, heard of the terrible things the Queen had done to his daughter, he banished her from his land forever. Before long, Snow White and her Prince were married. But she never forgot the kindness the seven dwarfs had shown her for the rest of her life.

Cinderella

There once lived a man who had a kind and pretty wife and a beautiful daughter. Sadly, the man's wife died soon after their daughter was born. A few years later, the man decided to marry again. His second wife was not kind and pretty, and she already had two daughters who were even less kind and pretty than she was. In fact, her daughters were so selfish, proud and greedy that they were known as the "ugly sisters".

From the first day they moved in, the ugly sisters were cruel and unkind to their stepsister. They spent all day doing nothing but gossiping and buying new dresses and trying to make themselves look pretty. Meanwhile, they made their poor stepsister do all the housework. She had to clean the house from top to bottom, do all the cooking, wash and scour the pots and pans and clear out the cinders from the fireplace. She spent so much time doing this that her stepsisters called her "Cinderella". Soon, poor Cinderella was tired out from working so hard. She began to look pale and thin, and her one dress started to look ragged and dirty.

One day, the King and Queen decided to hold a grand ball. Everyone in the town was hoping for an invitation, especially the two ugly sisters who each secretly thought that they might be able to marry the Prince. They couldn't believe their luck when, the very next day, an invitation arrived. That afternoon, they went on a huge shopping trip and came back with bags full of dresses, shoes and make-up. For the next few days, all they did was try on their new clothes. They couldn't decide what to wear for the ball.

When the big night arrived, the ugly sisters were still unsure what to wear, so they paraded their new clothes in front of poor Cinderella and asked her to tell them what suited them best.

"What a pity you're not invited to the ball, Cinders," one of them smirked to Cinderella.

"She's got nothing to wear," giggled the other one. "She couldn't possibly come in that old rag."

"Poor Cinderella," said the first one. "Never mind. We'll tell you all about it when we come back."

And with those words, they both swept out of the door and into their waiting carriage.

"Bye . . . Cinders," they both waved, leaning out of the carriage door. "Make sure the house is clean and neat for our return."

The carriage sped off into the night, whisking the excited ugly sisters to the ball, leaving poor Cinderella all alone.

After they'd left, Cinderella sat on the little stool near the fire.

"Why are my sisters so cruel to me?" she thought. "I do everything they tell me to do around the house, and more! They never thank me for it, or give me a kind word, or even smile at me." She felt so unhappy she began to cry. She would have loved one night of happiness at the ball.

Suddenly, a beautiful woman, carrying a silver wand, appeared right in front of her. She seemed to have come from nowhere.

"Who are you?" gasped Cinderella, a little frightened.

"Don't be scared. I am your Fairy Godmother," said the beautiful woman. "What's the matter, child? Why are you crying?"

"I would have loved to have gone to the ball," wept Cinderella. "But my stepsisters don't want me to go. Even if they did, I have nothing to wear and no carriage to take me there."

"Don't worry," said her Fairy Godmother, kindly. "This is your special day, Cinderella. You shall go to the ball! But, first, I'd like you to bring me some things. I need a pumpkin, two mice and the biggest rat you can find."

Cinderella rushed around the house and looked in all the mouse and rat traps. Soon there was a pumpkin, along with two little white mice in a box and a large rat, scurrying around in its cage, all lying at the Fairy Godmother's feet. With one wave of her silver wand, the Fairy Godmother changed the pumpkin into a golden coach, the mice into two magnificent white horses and the rat into a coachman.

Cinderella was astonished, and then looked down at her terrible dress. "But I can't go to the ball in this," she cried.

With another wave of her wand, the Fairy Godmother changed Cinderella's ragged dress into a ball gown made of the finest satin and silver thread. On her feet were a pair of beautiful glass slippers.

"Now, go and enjoy yourself," said the Fairy Godmother. "But be sure to be back before midnight, for when the clock strikes twelve everything will return to what it was before."

Cinderella stepped into the glistening carriage and was whisked through the dark streets until she reached the palace.

When she entered the ballroom, everyone stopped what they were doing and stared. They had never seen such a beautiful girl before. The Prince fell in love with her as soon as he saw her, and danced with her all evening. Cinderella thought that he was the most handsome man she had ever seen and fell in love with him, too. Cinderella was having such a wonderful time, she forgot all about her Fairy Godmother's warning. All of a sudden, she heard the clock strike twelve.

"Oh, no," she thought, "I must leave!"
She tore herself from the Prince's arms and rushed out of the ballroom. Before she reached the palace gates at the end of the drive, her beautiful dress had already turned back into the shabby, dirty dress that she always wore.

Back in the ballroom, the Prince couldn't understand why this lovely girl had suddenly run away. He searched the Palace for her, but couldn't find her anywhere. But, in her rush to leave, Cinderella had left behind one of her glass slippers. When the Prince found it on the Palace steps, he immediately issued a proclamation, saying that he intended to find and marry the girl whose foot fitted the glass slipper. He would visit every house in the land, until he had found her.

The ugly sisters became very excited. On the day that the Prince was going to visit their house, they made sure to wear their best dresses.

When the Prince arrived, he held out the glass slipper and asked which one of the sisters would like to try it on first.

"I will!" cried one of them. But, as much as she tried to push and, squeeze her foot into the slipper, it just wouldn't fit. Her foot was far too big.

"Give it to me!" said the other sister and, grabbing the slipper, tried to put it on. But her foot was far too big, too. However much she pushed and tugged, she just couldn't get her foot into it.

Just then, Cinderella stepped forward. She had been standing quietly in the shadows and no one had noticed her.

"May I try?" she asked, shyly.

"You!" cried the ugly sisters. "Of course you can't! Now get back to the kitchen where you belong!"

"Be quiet!" ordered the Prince. "Of course you may," he said, turning to Cinderella, not recognizing her. Cinderella sat down and put the slipper onto her foot. There was no pushing or pulling. It glided on perfectly. The ugly sisters gasped in amazement.

"I recognize you now," said the Prince, smiling. "You are the girl I fell in love with at the ball, and you are the girl I am going to marry."

"I can't believe this is happening," cried Cinderella. "I loved you the moment I met you, and I thought I'd never see you again."

Cinderella and the prince had a glorious wedding. She forgave her sisters their cruelty, and she never had to wash up a dirty dish ever again.

The Gingerbread Man

nce upon a time there was an old woman who decided to make some gingerbread. As she rolled out the dough, she noticed that she had a little bit left over.

"I'll make a gingerbread man out of this," she thought.

She cut the shape of a man out of the dough and used raisins for his eyes, nose and mouth.

"I'd better give him a jacket to wear," she thought. So she put raisins all down his front for buttons, too.

"There! That's not too bad," she said, looking at the little man proudly.

Then she put him in the oven to bake, alongside the gingerbread.

A short time later, she heard a strange scratching sound coming from inside the oven and a little voice crying, "Help! Let me out of here!"

She opened the oven door and, to her enormous surprise, out jumped the little gingerbread man.

"Thanks," he said. "It was getting very hot in there!"

Then he ran out of the kitchen door.

"Stop! Come back!" cried the old woman, chasing after him.

But the gingerbread man was far too quick for her. He looked back over his shoulder and said:

"Run, run, as fast as you can.
You can't catch me, I'm the gingerbread man!"

He ran into the garden where the old woman's husband was working.
"Stop!" cried the old woman's husband and, with his arms outstretched,
tried to grab the gingerbread man as he ran by. But the gingerbread
man was far too quick for him, and said:

"Run, run, as fast as you can.
You can't catch me, I'm the gingerbread man!"

He ran further along the lane with the old woman and her husband
chasing him.
Soon, he passed a cow who was eating some grass.
"Stop!' cried the cow. "Come back! You look good enough to eat!"
But the gingerbread man simply ran under the cow's legs and said:

"I've run from an old woman
and an old man.
Run, run, as fast as you can.
You can't catch me, I'm the gingerbread man!"

He ran further down the lane with the old woman, her husband and the cow chasing him.

A little later, he came across a horse in a field.

"Stop!' cried the horse. "Come back! You look good enough to eat!"

With one huge leap, the gingerbread man simply jumped right over the horse and laughed:

"I've run from an old woman
and an old man.
And a cow!
Run, run, as fast as you can.
You can't catch me, I'm the gingerbread man!"

He ran even further down the lane with the old woman,
her husband the cow and the horse chasing him.
When he passed some farmers making hay, they too cried,
"Stop! Come back! You look good enough to eat!"
But when they tried to grab him, the gingerbread man simply dived into
the pile of hay and came running out the other side.

"I've run from an old woman
and an old man.
And a cow and a horse!
Run, run, as fast as you can.
You can't catch me, I'm the gingerbread man!"

He ran much further down the lane, and then into a field, with the old woman, her husband, the cow, the horse and the farmers all chasing him! At the bottom of the field he met a fox and said to him:

"Run, run, as fast as you can.
You can't catch me, I'm the gingerbread man!"

But the fox was a sly, old thing who realized that he would have to be patient if he was going to catch the gingerbread man.

Soon after, the gingerbread man came to a river.

"Quick!" said the fox, who leapt out from behind a bush. "Jump on my back and I'll take you across, otherwise they'll catch you!"

The gingerbread man hopped onto the fox's back who then started to swim across the river. When they were halfway across, the water suddenly got deeper.

"You'd better sit on my head if you don't want to get wet!" the fox told the gingerbread man.

The gingerbread man did as he was told and hopped onto the fox's head.

A little further on, the water got deeper still.

"You'd better sit on my nose if you don't want to get wet!" said the fox to the gingerbread man.

The gingerbread man did as he was told and hopped onto the fox's nose. And that was the gingerbread man's big mistake. For as soon as he sat on the fox's nose, the fox opened his mouth, went snap and gobbled up the little gingerbread man straight away.

And, sadly, that was the end of the gingerbread man.

Three Little Pigs

Once upon a time there was an old sow who had three little piglets. When they were old enough, she told them that they should leave home and make their own way in the world. The first little pig met a man carrying a large bundle of straw. The pig thought that a house made of straw would make a very fine house indeed. So he bought the straw from the man and, in no time at all, had built himself a house. The house looked very nice, but wasn't very strong.

One day, a hungry wolf came passing by and saw the pig sitting in his house, enjoying a cup of tea.

"What a nice pig," he thought. "He would fill me up."

So he went and knocked on the door. "Little pig, little pig, let me come in," said the wolf.

"Not by the hair of my chinny chin chin!" said the frightened pig.

"Then I'll huff, and I'll puff, and I'll blow your house down!" cried the wolf.

Then he huffed, and he puffed, and he blew down the little pig's house

of straw. Instantly, the wolf was at the pig's side and he gobbled him up.
Meanwhile, the second little pig had met a man who was carrying a
large pile of sticks.

"Those are just the sort of sticks I need to build myself a house,"
thought the pig.

He bought the sticks and, after working very hard, had soon built
himself a house. The house looked very nice, but wasn't very strong.

Not long after, the wolf passed by and noticed the pig sitting at his window, enjoying a slice of cake.

"Another pig!" he thought. "I'm in luck!"

He went and knocked on the front door.

"Little pig, little pig, let me come in," said the wolf.

"Not by the hair of my chinny chin chin!" said the frightened pig.

"Then I'll huff, and I'll puff, and I'll blow your house down!" cried the wolf.

Then he huffed, and he puffed, and he blew down the little pig's house of sticks.

In one bound, the wolf was at the pig's side and he ate him all up.

"Two pigs in one week," thought the wolf, licking his lips.

"Life can't get much better than this!"

The third little pig had also met a man, and that man was carrying a large load of bricks.

"These bricks would make a strong house for me to live in," thought the pig. So he bought the bricks, and soon had built himself a house. The house looked very nice, and was very strong.

One day, the wolf passed by and saw the pig eating an apple pie.
"Another pig," thought the wolf. "Hooray!"
He went and knocked on the door. "Little pig, little pig, let me come in."
"Not by the hair of my chinny chin chin!" said the pig, who was not at
all frightened and just carried on eating his apple pie.
"Then I'll huff, and I'll puff, and I'll blow your house down!" cried
the wolf.
Well, the wolf huffed, and he puffed, and tried to blow the house down
but, it was so strong, it didn't move at all. The wolf tried harder and
huffed and puffed with all his might, but the house still wouldn't
fall down.
The wolf decided to try to trick the pig out of his house.
"Oh, little piggy," the wolf shouted through the door. "There are some

lovely turnips growing in the field next door. Why don't you and I get up bright and early tomorrow morning and go pick some?"

"What a good idea," said the pig. "See you here at seven o'clock."

But the clever pig got to the field at six o'clock and picked all the turnips he needed. By the time the wolf arrived at seven o'clock, the pig was safely back in his house again.

The wolf was very angry that the pig had fooled him, but he had another trick up his sleeve.

"Oh, little piggy," he shouted. "There are some juicy ripe apples just waiting to be picked in the orchard down the road. Why don't we meet there this afternoon and pick some together?"

"What a good idea," said the pig. "See you there after lunch."

But when the wolf arrived at the orchard, the little pig was already up an apple tree. When he saw the wolf, the pig threw an apple as far as he could. While the wolf chased after it, the pig quickly climbed down the tree, got into a barrel and rolled all the way home.

When the wolf realized that the pig had tricked him again, he was

furious. He was so angry, he walked all the way back to the pig's house and climbed onto the roof. He decided to climb down the chimney to catch the pig. But the clever pig had placed a large pot of boiling water in his fireplace. The wolf came down the chimney and fell straight into the pot of boiling water! The pig quickly put on the lid, and that evening sat down to a lovely meal of boiled wolf with turnips from the field next door. He finished his meal off with a big, juicy apple from the orchard down the road. What a very clever pig he was.

The Princess and The Pea

In a distant land, there lived a Prince who decided one day, that he wanted nothing more in the world than to marry a beautiful Princess. His parents, the King and Queen, agreed that he was now old enough to marry and wished him well in his hunt.

For the next two years he journeyed far and wide to find his perfect wife. But the Prince was a very choosy person and, although he met lots of Princesses along the way, he always found something wrong with them. They were either too short or too tall. Too fat or too thin. Too happy or too sad, or just too nice!

When he returned home, he was very upset that he couldn't find the right Princess to marry.

"There, there," said the Queen, comforting her son. "I know it must be terribly upsetting for you, dear, but I'm sure that the right Princess will come along one day."

"But I might be an old man by the time that happens," moaned the unfortunate Prince.

"Now," said his father, the King, "things aren't that bad. You're still young, rich, handsome and a Prince! You're bound to find the right girl soon."

"But, when?" cried the Prince.

In truth, the King and Queen were a bit fed up with their son (who was acting a bit spoiled) and decided to send him away to one of their other castles for a complete rest.

One night, there was a terrible storm. Thunder and lightening filled the
sky. The windows rattled and the wind whistled around the rooms of
the old castle.

As the storm raged on, there was a knock on the huge castle door.
The Queen opened it and standing before her was a young girl who was
shivering from the cold and the rain.

"My goodness," said the Queen. "What a dreadful night to be outside. You're soaked through, my dear. You'd better come in and we'll find you some dry clothes."
"How kind of you," said the girl.

The Queen led her to the drawing room where she could dry herself by the large, crackling fire.
"Do you live nearby?" asked the Queen.
"No, Your Majesty," replied the girl. "I'm a Princess from another land. My carriage is stuck in the mud, a little way down the road."

As the Queen and the girl talked, the Queen began to realize that this young Princess might make the perfect wife for her son. She wasn't too short or too tall. She wasn't too fat or too thin. She wasn't too happy or too sad and, although she seemed very nice, she didn't seem to be too nice. But the Queen wanted to make sure the girl was a real Princess so that they wouldn't be disappointed. She had an idea how she could find out.

"My dear," said the Queen. "We can't possibly let you leave on such a terrible night as this. I insist that you stay here tonight. I will get the maids to make up a bed in one of the guest bed-chambers."
"That's very kind of you, Your Majesty," said the girl, who gave a little curtsy, and went off to have a steaming hot bath.

The Queen told her maids to collect as many mattresses and quilts as they could find and to stack them on the guest's bed. Then, she went to the castle kitchen where she picked out a single, dried pea from a jar. She gave the pea to one of the maids, and ordered that it be placed underneath the bottom mattress.

The girl's bed was now so tall she had to use a ladder to get into it!

In the morning, the Queen asked the girl if she'd had a good night's sleep.
"Not really," replied the girl. "There was an annoying little lump in my bed that kept me awake all night."
This was just the reply that the Queen had been hoping for. Only a real Princess would have been able to feel a pea under all those mattresses and quilts.

When the Queen introduced her son to the Princess, they liked each other immediately.
"She's neither too short or too tall," the Prince told his parents. "Too fat or too thin. Too happy or too sad, or just plain old too nice! In fact, she's just perfect for me."

The Prince and the Princess got married, and the pea was put in a special case in the town's museum. For many years, the local people delighted in telling visitors the famous story of the Princess and the pea.

Beauty and The Beast

Long ago, there lived a rich merchant who had three sons and three daughters. Unfortunately, his sons were only interested in hunting and fishing, while his two eldest daughters were greedy and selfish. Only his youngest daughter liked by everyone. Everyone called her "Beauty". Not only was she very beautiful to look at, she but was the kindest person that anyone had ever met.

One day, the merchant heard some terrible news. All the ships carrying his goods had sunk at sea in a storm, which left him with hardly any money. The whole family had to move from their grand house to a little cottage. While the merchant and his sons worked hard all day in the fields, his daughters stayed at home doing the housework. The two eldest daughters were very lazy and sat around doing nothing. Beauty, however, enjoyed her work around the cottage, happy to be helping her father in these difficult times.

One morning, a letter arrived for the merchant. It said that one of his ships had not sunk and it was going to arrive at the port the following morning.
"Maybe we're not so poor, after all!" said the merchant, happily. With great excitement, he set off to meet his ship. Before he left, he asked his daughters what they would like as gifts. The eldest daughters asked for jewels and beautiful clothes but Beauty, who didn't have a greedy bone in her body, simply asked for a single red rose.

When the merchant got to the port he found out that there had been
a terrible mistake. There was no ship coming into port, which meant
that he was just as poor as before. The unhappy man turned his horse
around and set off for home again.

Later that night, there was a huge storm. Thunder and lightening filled
the sky, and the poor merchant lost his way in the darkness. He was
soon soaked to the skin and his horse was getting very tired.
At last, he saw lights in the distance. Getting closer, he realized that the
lights shone from a castle. He rode up to the castle, and knocked on the
door. It creaked open.

Inside, he found a roaring fire and food on the table, but only one plate. There was no one else around, so he sat down and ate. After he'd eaten, he went outside and discovered a stable in the courtyard. It was bright and warm with lots of hay for his horse to eat and clean straw for it to sleep on. Back in the castle, he ventured upstairs. One of the bedrooms was warm, with freshly ironed sheets laid out on the bed.

"It's almost as if I was expected," thought the merchant, before climbing into bed and falling fast asleep.

When he awoke the next morning, he got dressed and went downstairs. Again, breakfast was neatly laid out on the table. Again, nobody else was around. After he'd eaten, he saddled his horse. Riding out of the long drive, he noticed a rosebush with beautiful, red flowers.

"At least I can give Beauty the present she asked for," he thought, and plucked a single red rose from the bush.

From out of the bushes, an ugly looking Beast appeared in front of him. "You eat my food, sleep in my guest room and now you want to steal one of my roses. You shall die for this!"

The terrified merchant stuttered back, "But I didn't see anyone to thank. And I was only taking this one rose for Beauty."

"Who is this Beauty?" demanded the Beast.

"She is my daughter," replied the merchant.

The Beast thought for a moment.

"Very well, then," he said. "You may leave here on the condition that your daughter, Beauty, takes your place and comes to me here."

The merchant was so scared, he hastily agreed and rode out of the castle grounds as quickly as possible.

When he arrived home, he told his family what had happened.

"I can't possibly let you go," he told Beauty through his tears. "The Beast might kill you!"

"You have to, father," said Beauty calmly. "If I don't go, he might take revenge on our family."

Sadly, the merchant agreed that he had to let Beauty go. With a heavy heart, he waved her farewell as she set out for the Beast's castle.

When she got there, she found to her great surprise that the Beast was very kind to her. He showed her around the castle and its beautiful grounds and then took her to her room. The Beast had made sure that all the books she'd like to read and all the little ornaments she'd like to look at were there. There was even a magic mirror in which she could see her family back at home. The scene lasted a few seconds before it faded away.

"This Beast may be ugly, but he is very considerate," thought Beauty.

On that first evening, the Beast came to eat supper with her. After
the meal, he asked her to marry him.

"I'm sorry, but I cannot marry you," she replied.

The Beast sighed, and then slowly walked out of the room.

From then on, it was the same every evening. Beauty and the Beast
would have supper together and then he'd ask her to marry him. Beauty
always gave the same reply: "I'm sorry, but I cannot marry you."

Time passed. Then, one evening, Beauty looked into the mirror and saw that her father was very ill. She begged the Beast to allow her to go home and care for him.

"Very well," said the Beast. "But you must return here within a week. When you are ready to come back, put this ring on your dressing table at home and I shall know you want to return here. If you don't do this within one week, I shall die."

Beauty agreed, and when she woke up the next morning, she found herself in her own bed at home.

She cared for her father day and night over the next few days, and soon one week had passed. Although her father was getting better, Beauty had been so busy, she hadn't noticed how quickly the days had passed. To make matters worse, her older sisters who had always been jealous of her, didn't tell her. They were secretly hoping that the longer she stayed at home, the angrier the Beast would become.

"He might even kill her!" they chuckled to themselves.

One night, Beauty had a dream that the Beast was lying dead by the side of the lake in his castle grounds.

"I must go back to him," she thought. She put the ring he gave her on her dressing table, and the next morning found herself back in his castle. She ran down to the lake and was horrified to see that the Beast was lying on the ground, barely alive.

"Oh, Beast," she cried, "I did not mean to stay away so long. Please come back to me. You are so good and kind."

Then, she kissed him.

Suddenly, the Beast changed right in front of her eyes. All signs of his ugliness had disappeared and there was a handsome prince in his place. "Beauty, my love," explained the Prince. "I had a spell cast on me many years ago that turned me into an ugly beast. The only way it could be broken was if a girl who loved me, kissed me in spite of my ugliness." Beauty kissed him again and vowed that she would stay by his side forever.

The happy couple rode to her father's house where they were married. Then they journeyed back to the castle where they lived in complete happiness for many years to come.

Sleeping Beauty

There once were a King and Queen who seemed to have everything anyone could wish for. They lived in a beautiful palace and ruled over a happy country where all their subjects loved them dearly. But there was one thing that made the King and Queen very sad indeed: they had no children.

One morning, as the King was looking over some documents with his courtiers, the Queen suddenly burst in.

"My dear," she said breathlessly, "I have great news!"

"And what might that be, my love?" asked the King.

"I'm going to have a baby!" exclaimed the Queen, excitedly.

The King was so delighted he dropped his map, burst into tears and gave his wife a great big hug.

A few months later, the Queen gave birth to a little girl. And she was the prettiest baby anyone had ever seen. She had big blue eyes, lovely blonde hair and a perfect smile. The King was so taken with his child, he ordered a national holiday on the day she was born. He and the Queen adored their new daughter and spent many hours gazing lovingly at her.

"She's as beautiful as you, my dear," said the King fondly to the Queen.

"I'm sure she'll grow up to be as wise as you," the Queen replied.

"Thank you, my love. How blessed we are," said the King.

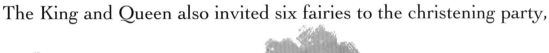

The King decided to hold a huge christening party for the new Princess, and invited people from far and wide. When the great day came, everyone in the palace was very excited. The cooks had been up all night preparing delicious food, the royal gardeners had been working for weeks to make the palace grounds look perfect and the sentries had polished their buttons so hard, they gleamed like gold.

Everybody had a wonderful time! After the great feast, the King clapped his hands and the music and dancing began.

The King and Queen also invited six fairies to the christening party,

whom they hoped would bestow special gifts on the new Princess.

When all the guests had exhausted themselves on the dance floor, it was time for the fairies to bestow their gifts on the newborn Princess. One by one, they approached her crib.

"I bestow beauty on you," said the first fairy, gazing fondly down at the gurgling Princess.

"Joy," said the second.

"Wisdom," said the third.

"To be generous," said the fourth.

"Health," said the fifth.

But before the sixth fairy could bestow her gifts, the doors of the great chamber were suddenly flung open. There stood an old, ugly fairy that no one really liked, and were secretly a little afraid of.

"Why wasn't I invited to your party?" the old fairy asked, glaring at the King.

"Well … I … umm, I'm not quite sure," stuttered the King, looking down at his shoes, feeling embarrassed.

Everyone fell silent.

"I have a gift I'd like to bestow on the dear child." said the old fairy, walking up to the crib and looking down at the Princess.

"My gift to you," she began, "is that when you reach the age of sixteen, you will prick yourself on the spindle of spinning wheel and you will die!"

And with that, she turned around and walked angrily out of the palace.

The poor Queen burst into tears. Then a lovely, clear voice rang out. It was the sixth fairy.

"I haven't bestowed my gift yet," she said.

"I can not undo the terrible curse of the old fairy but I can change it a little. My gift to you, little one, is that you won't die if you prick your finger on a spindle but, instead, you will sleep for one hundred years."

From that day on, the King banned all use of spinning wheels. If people wanted any wool to be spun, they had to send it to another land.

Time passed, and everyone started to forget the old fairy and her curse. The Princess grew up to be beautiful, healthy, wise and generous. Everyone in the country loved her.
On her sixteenth birthday, the King gave a grand party. For a present,

he had a beautiful dress made for her. It was the first proper grown up dress the Princess had ever worn. It was a lovely, green silk dress, with an elegant, high collar, and it was so long it reached the floor.

The Princess invited all her friends to the party. After eating a huge birthday lunch, they decided to play hide-and-seek.
"You won't catch me," said the Princess, running quickly away.
Trying to find a place where nobody would find her, she climbed a stone staircase to the very top of one of the palace's towers.

At the top was a small room. Inside the room, an old lady sat at her spinning wheel. She had been there for years, and hadn't heard that spinning wheels had been banned long ago.

"How nice to see you, my dear," said the old lady with a warm smile.

"What beautiful thread you're making!" exclaimed the Princess. "May I try the spinning wheel?"

She sat down at the wheel and began to spin but, as soon as she did so, the spindle pricked her finger.

With a small cry, she fell to the ground and fell fast asleep.

At that very moment, everybody else in the palace, and in the palace grounds, fell asleep too.

Many years went by and, little by little, a huge thorn hedge grew

around the palace. It was so thick that the few people who tried to fight their way through gave up. In time, the palace, and the people sleeping in it, were completely forgotten.

Then, one day, a Prince from a far off land rode by and saw one of the palace's gleaming towers in the distance. In a nearby village, he asked if anybody knew to whom it belonged. But nobody did. It was too long ago. Then, a very old man said his grandfather had told him that, many years ago, a palace had stood there, but no one had been able to cut through the thorn hedge to get to it.

This story made the Prince curious, and he decided to try to cut through the dense hedge. He took out his sword, and started to hack his way through the thorns. Without warning, the thorn bush suddenly fell back, and cleared a path for him right up to the palace itself.

To his great surprise, the Prince saw people draped all around the grounds. They all seemed to be sleeping. The Prince warily made his way into the Palace. It was exactly the same inside: people everywhere, and they were all fast asleep! Treading carefully, the Prince slowly made his way up the grand staircase, passing sleeping people as he went. At the top of the stairs was a large oak door. He pushed it open and

couldn't believe his eyes. In front of him lay a lovely Princess who was also sound asleep. She was so beautiful, he gasped out loud. In one swift movement, the Prince knelt by her side and kissed her gently on the lips. To his utter astonishment, her eyes slowly opened, and she began to wake. The Prince looked into her deep blue eyes and realized she was the girl he had been waiting for all his life.

At that moment, everyone else in the palace woke up, too. It was exactly one hundred years since the old fairy had cast her evil curse. When they realized what had happened all those years before, everyone was so happy to be alive.

The Prince and Princess decided to marry. The palace was cleaned of its cobwebs and their wedding took place soon after. It was a joyous day for everyone and the Prince and Princess lived happily ever after.

Rumpelstiltskin

Once upon a time there was on old woman who lived with her beautiful daughter in a run-down old cottage. The woman and the girl were very poor and it was always hard to find enough to eat. One day, the old woman happened to see the King riding along the road by her cottage.

"If only I could arrange for the King to meet my daughter," she thought. "She's so beautiful, he might even marry her."

She grabbed hold of the King's horse and pulled it to a stop.

"Please, sire, you must meet my daughter. She is very beautiful."

"You stupid woman. Get out of my way before I whip you!" cried the King, nearly falling off his horse.

"But she can do something that would make you very rich," the woman said, desperately trying to hold his attention.

"Oh, and what is that?" asked the King, with curiosity.

The old woman said the first thing that came into her head.

"She can spin straw into gold," she lied.

The King took the old woman's daughter, whose name was Rose, to his castle. He locked her up in a small room that was full of straw. The only other things in the room were a spinning wheel and a small stool.

"Listen to me, Rose," the King began. "I will return in the morning. If all this straw has not been turned into gold, I will chop your pretty little head off. Good night!" Then he walked out of the room, locking the door behind him.

Poor Rose was so afraid she started to cry. Just then, she noticed a funny little man with a long, grey beard standing at her elbow.

"What's the matter, my dear?" asked the funny little man.

"My stupid mother told the King that I can spin straw into gold," cried Rose. If I can't do it, the King will have my head chopped off . . . and I can't do it!"

"I can," said the funny little man. "What would you give me if I did it for you?"

"My necklace," replied Rose, taking it from her neck.

"That will do fine," said the little man, putting it in his pocket. "You have a rest and I'll get on with my work."

The little man sat down and started to spin. The last thing Rose heard before she fell asleep was the whirr of the spinning wheel as it went round and round and round.

The next morning, with the sun streaming in through the window, Rose awoke. She rubbed her eyes and couldn't believe what she saw. There was no sign of the funny little man but all the straw in the room had been turned into the finest gold. The King was very pleased when he saw it all.

"You've done very well, Rose," he said. "Now, come with me."

This time he took her to an even bigger room which, again, was full of straw.

"I want all of this spun into gold by the morning or I'll chop your head off!" threatened the King.

Once again, he left Rose alone in the room and locked the door behind him.

"What am I going to do?" thought Rose, and she began to cry again.

"Don't cry," said a voice at her elbow. "I'll turn it all into gold for you. But what will you give me in return?"

It was the funny little man again, who had just appeared from nowhere!

"Here, take my ring. It was my grandmother's," said Rose, pulling it off her finger.

The little man put the ring in his pocket, sat at the wheel and began to spin.

The next morning, it was the same as before. The little man had gone and all of the straw had been turned into gold. When the King saw this, he took Rose to a very large room that had straw piled up to the ceiling. "If you manage to turn all of this into gold, I'll make you my Queen," he said. "If you don't, it's off with your head!"

After the King had left, the funny little man appeared once more, and once more offered to turn all the straw into gold.

"But I have nothing left to give you," said poor Rose.

"There is one thing you can give me. You can give me your first born baby," said the little man, slyly. "If you make me this promise, I will turn all of this straw into gold."

Rose was so desperate, she agreed to his demand at once.

When the King saw the huge amount of gold in the room the next morning, he was so pleased that he married Rose immediately. A year later, she gave birth to a lovely, little baby boy.

In time, Rose forgot about her promise to the little man but, one evening, when she was all alone nursing her baby, he suddenly appeared at her elbow.

"I have come to claim the baby you promised me," he said, with a cold look in his eye.

Rose was horrified and promised the little man anything he wanted: jewels, gold, anything. As long as he didn't take her child away.

The little man thought for a moment and then said, "I will give you a chance to keep your child. I will come here for the next three nights and each night I will give you three chances to guess my name. If you don't guess correctly by the third night, you will never see your baby again."

When the little man appeared on the first night, Rose tried to think of three of the most unusual names.

"Is it Caspar?" she asked.

"No," replied the little man.

"Is it Balthasar?" she asked, anxiously.

"I'm afraid not," he replied with an evil grin.

"What about Melchior?" she asked, even more anxiously.

"Wrong, wrong, wrong!" he cried, gleefully. Then he stamped his foot and disappeared.

The next evening, Rose thought that she'd try more ordinary names.

"Is it John?"

"No," replied the little man.

"Arthur?" she asked again.

"Not even close," he replied.

"How about George?" asked Rose.

"Wrong, wrong, wrong again!" he shouted, happily.

Once again, Rose had failed.

The little man was so pleased that Rose couldn't guess his name, he started to dance around the room with joy.

"If you don't guess my name tomorrow night," he cried, "the child is mine!" Then he stamped his foot and disappeared.

Early the next morning, Rose sent all her servants out to see if they
could find anyone who had heard of the little man and knew his name.
One by one the servants came back. They could find no one who had
heard of him. Finally, the last servant arrived back and had a strange
tale to tell Rose.

"I was riding through the forest," he said, "and I saw a strange little
man with a long, grey beard dancing around his fire. He sang a strange
song, too."

"Today I brew, tomorrow I bake.
Next day, Queen Rose's baby I'll take.
So I solemnly swear by the hair on my chin,
That the name I was given is Rumpelstiltskin."

Rose was so delighted with this news, she gave the servant a large bag
of gold coins as a reward. Later that evening, the little man once again
appeared in front of her.

"What are your last three guesses?" he asked Rose, smugly.

"Is it Karl?" she asked.

"No," he replied, happily.

"Umm . . . Richard?" she asked again.

"Nowhere near, I'm afraid. It's your last guess, Your Majesty, and then
the child is mine," the little man said, menacingly.

"Is it . . . Rumpelstiltskin?" asked Rose, innocently.

The little man was so angry that Rose had guessed his name, he turned
bright blue. He stamped his foot down so hard that he went right
through the floor, and that was the end of Rumpelstiltskin.

Hansel and Gretel

There was once a woodcutter and his wife who lived in a tiny cottage, on the edge of a magnificent forest, with their two children. They had a boy called Hansel and a girl called Gretel. It was a hard life and there never seemed to be enough food.

In one particularly lean year, the woodcutter's wife turned to her husband one night. "There's not enough bread for us all tomorrow," she said. "It would be best for everyone if you took the children into the forest and left them there."
"But they'll starve to death!" exclaimed the woodcutter.
"It's either them or us," replied his heartless wife.
The woodcutter tried to make his wife change her mind, but after much argument, he reluctantly agreed to leave his children in the forest the following day.

Meanwhile, Hansel had overheard his mother and father arguing. When he heard of their terrible plan, he crept outside, picked up some white pebbles and put them in his pocket. Early the next morning, the woodcutter told his children that they must help carry the wood that he was going to chop down that day. As they walked deeper into the forest, Hansel began to drop behind him the pebbles he had collected.
"What are you doing?" Gretel asked him.

"Sshh! You'll find out," replied her brother.

After walking for many hours, the woodcutter told his children to rest while he started to cut down the trees. The children were tired after walking so far and slowly drifted off to sleep on the forest floor. When they awoke, it was night, and very dark. They realized that their father

had left them in the forest, completely alone.

"I'm frightened," said Gretel, clutching her brother's arm.

"Don't worry," said Hansel. "Do you remember those white pebbles I dropped on the way here? If we follow them, they'll lead us home." Sure enough, the children followed the trail of white pebbles that gleamed in the dark, and they arrived home just as the sun had started to lighten the sky.

Their father was overjoyed to see them and hugged them tightly. He hadn't wanted to leave them in the forest in the first place. But their mother was not at all pleased to see them, and packed them off to bed as quickly as possible. That night, she told her husband that the next day he was to take the children even further into the forest and leave them there again. The poor woodcutter tried to argue with her but she refused to change her mind.

Early the next morning, Hansel and Gretel's mother gave them each a chunk of bread and told them that they must help their father in the forest again. This time, clever Hansel tore off little bits of the bread and dropped them behind him as they walked along the path.

"See," he whispered to his sister. "If father leaves us in the forest again, we'll be able to follow the bits of bread all the way back home."

"You are clever, Hansel," said Gretel.

Once again, the woodcutter urged his children to rest as he began his work. They were so tired, they soon fell into a long sleep.

When the children woke up, they realized that their father had left them again. They were all alone in the cold, frightening forest.

"What are we going to do?" asked Gretel, nervously.

"We'll just follow the bits of bread, as I told you," Hansel replied, shivering a little from the cold. "Don't worry, everything will be fine." But as hard as they looked, the children couldn't find any pieces of bread, anywhere!

"Oh no!" cried Hansel. "The birds must have eaten it all. That's why we can't find any pieces of bread,"

That night, it was so cold it was impossible to keep still. The children walked around the forest, trying to keep warm, hoping that they wouldn't bump into a large, hungry animal. As the sun started to come up, they saw a white bird in the sky that seemed to be beckoning to them. Having no other plan, they followed the bird, which led them to a little cottage. They were amazed to see that the cottage walls were made entirely out of bread, the roof was iced ginger cake and the windows were made of sparkling sugar. Hansel and Gretel were so hungry they

immediately began to tear bits of bread off the walls and ravenously started to eat it.

Just then, a little voice rang out:

"Nibble, nibble, little mouse,

Who's that nibbling at my house?"

Then the door opened and a little old lady came out. Hansel and Gretel thought they might be punished for eating bits of her house but the old lady simply smiled and said, "My goodness! You children must be hungry. Come inside and I'll make you breakfast."

The old lady seemed very kind, and made Hansel and Gretel a delicious breakfast.

Then she showed them to a tidy, little bedroom that had two comfortable beds in it, where they could have a lovely, long sleep.

126

"Aren't we lucky to have found this kind lady?" said Gretel as she got into bed.

But the kind old lady was not a kind old lady at all. She was, in fact, a horrible, nasty witch who enjoyed roasting children in her oven so that she could eat them!

The next morning, the cruel witch locked Hansel in a large cage with bars all around, and told Gretel to cook food for her brother.

"He needs fattening up before he's ready for my oven," she hissed to the poor girl.

Each day, the witch told Hansel to stick a finger through the bars so she could feel how fat he was getting. But Hansel was clever and, instead of poking out his finger, he stuck a little bone out, to make the witch think he wasn't putting on any weight at all!

After a month, the witch was getting impatient and decided to eat Hansel straight away. She ordered Gretel to make a fire in the oven, then told her to get into it to make sure it was hot enough. Poor Gretel knew that if she crawled into the oven, the witch would close the door behind her and roast her as well as her brother.

"I'm not very good at climbing into things. Could you show me how, please?" Gretel asked the witch.

"Oh, all right," said the witch, who opened the door and crawled inside the oven to show exactly how it should be done.

But, when the witch was halfway in, Gretel pushed her all the way with a great shove, and slammed the door shut behind her. And that was the end of a very horrible witch.

Gretel released her brother from the cage and together they searched the cottage for anything that might be useful. They were amazed to

find that the cottage was crammed full of gold coins, silver trinkets and precious jewels. They gathered it all up and began to search for the way home.

After wandering for a long time, they saw smoke rising from a chimney in the distance. They were overjoyed to see that it was their cottage. They had found their home, at last.

When their father saw that his children were alive and well, he dropped his axe and hugged them close to him.

"I'm so happy to see you both again," he cried.

"I thought you were dead, for sure!"

When he saw the treasure that they had brought with them, he couldn't believe his eyes.

Hansel and Gretel sold everything that they found in the witch's cottage and became very rich. Although their cruel mother had died while they were lost in the forest, the children and their father lived happily together for the rest of their days.

Aladdin's Lamp

A long time ago in faraway China, there lived a poor tailor, his wife and their son, Aladdin. The tailor worked hard and hoped that his son would one day enter the family business. But all Aladdin liked to do was spend time with his friends. Even when his father died, Aladdin didn't stop being lazy. It was left to his poor old mother to bring a little money into the house by spinning cotton.

One day, while he was lazing around as usual, a stranger approached Aladdin and said, "My goodness, but you must be Aladdin. You look just like your father! I am your father's brother who has been away for many years. Please take me to your mother at once."

Aladdin was surprised. He didn't think he had an uncle but did as he was told, anyway. When his mother saw the stranger she was also confused and said, "Yes, my husband did have a brother. I never met him. I thought he died many years ago."

But it was such a happy meeting and the stranger seemed such a nice man, she found it easy to believe that it was her dead husband's brother.

What Aladdin and his mother didn't know was that the stranger was an evil magician who had picked Aladdin because he looked like a wastrel. He wanted to use Aladdin for his own ends and then get rid of him. However, for the time being, he was very charming to the boy and his mother.

After treating them to a good meal, the magician told the boy he'd like to show him around the richer parts of the city. They walked through beautiful gardens and wide streets with magnificent houses. After a while, Aladdin and the magician found themselves in a small, dark alley. Without warning, the magician stopped and pulled on a big metal ring attached to a flat stone in the middle of the street. Underneath the stone were stairs, leading down into darkness.

"Nephew," began the magician. "You must go down these stairs for me. At the bottom you will find three caves full of gold and silver. You must pass through all of the caves and promise not to touch anything! Then you will enter a garden full of strange stone-fruit hanging from the trees. You may pick some of it if you wish. At the end of the garden you will find a dirty old lamp. Empty the oil from it and bring it to me. The lamp is the only thing I wish for."

Aladdin was a little nervous, but the magician had given him a beautiful emerald ring to keep if he promised to bring the lamp back. Aladdin went slowly down the stairs. At the bottom, he found the three caves that were full of gold and silver, just as his uncle had said. But he kept his promise and didn't touch any of it.

Then he entered the garden with the strange stone-fruit hanging from the trees. He stuffed as many as he could into his pockets, then carried on until he reached the end of the garden. There, he saw the old oil lamp. He picked it up, poured out the old, dirty oil and walked back through the garden and the three caves until he reached the stairs again.

The magician was waiting for him at the top of the stairs.

"Give me the lamp!" he said eagerly.

"Help me out of here first, and then I'll give you the lamp," said Aladdin.

"I want it now!" cried the magician, and tried to grab the lamp out of Aladdin's hand. This had been his plan all along. He was going to take the lamp, then shut Aladdin beneath the ground forever. But as the two of them struggled, the stone suddenly fell back over the hole, shutting Aladdin, with the lamp, firmly inside.

The magician quickly realized that his plan had failed, and left China, never to be seen again.

For two days Aladdin stayed in the cave without any food and water. He was getting very weak. Then, by chance, he rubbed the ring the magician had given him. All of a sudden, there was a blinding flash and a very large man appeared in front of him.

"Who are you?" asked Aladdin in astonishment.

"I am the Genie of the Ring, master. Your wish is my command. What can I do for you?"

"Get me out of here!" cried Aladdin.

There was another blinding flash and Aladdin found himself standing in the alley above. Looking down, he saw that the big metal ring and the flat stone had completely disappeared. He rushed home to his mother, who was overjoyed to see him.

"Where have you been, my boy?" she asked, hugging him.

"I'll tell you later," said Aladdin. "I'm so hungry. I haven't eaten for two days. Please feed me, mother."

His mother cooked up whatever bits she had in the house, but it wasn't very much and, after he'd finished eating, Aladdin was still hungry.

"Maybe I can sell the lamp for food," he said. "I'd better give it a polish."
As soon as he started to rub the lamp, there was another blinding flash
and another large man appeared!

Both Aladdin and his mother cried out in amazement.

"Who are you?" asked Aladdin in a trembling voice.

"I am the Genie of the Lamp, master," said the large man. "Your wish is
my command. What can I do for you?"

"Bring me a table full of food," commanded Aladdin.

In the blink of an eye, a table appeared crammed full of the most
delicious food, all served up on silver plates. When Aladdin and his
mother had eaten everything, they sold the silver plates for a lot of
money, which bought them enough food not to go hungry again for a
very long time.

One day, while strolling in the market, Aladdin saw the Sultan's
daughter, Princess Badroulboudoir, and fell in love with her instantly.
He went to see the Sultan and asked for his daughter's hand in
marriage. As a gift, Aladdin gave the Sultan all of the stone-fruit he'd
found hanging from the trees in the cave.

"You must be very rich to give me such a present," smiled the Sultan.
"You're exactly the sort of man I wish my daughter to marry."

But the Sultan's chief courtier wanted his son to marry the Princess, so
he urged the Sultan to give Aladdin a test to prove himself. So the Sultan
asked Aladdin for even more of the stone-fruit. But this time the Sultan
wanted forty servants to carry the fruit to his palace on forty
silver platters.

When he was alone, Aladdin once again rubbed the lamp, and again the
Genie appeared.

"What can I do for you, master?" he asked Aladdin.
"Send forty servants, bearing forty platters of stone-fruit, to the Sultan's palace," ordered Aladdin.

The Sultan was astonished when, the very next day, forty servants bearing forty platters of fruit arrived at his palace.
"Look at this!" exclaimed the Sultan. "I am now certain that Aladdin will make a fine husband for my daughter."
But the chief courtier, who still had hopes that his son might marry the Sultan's daughter, suggested one final test for Aladdin.
"This is all well and good," he said. "But where would they live if they were married? If Aladdin is as wealthy as he says he is, he should be able to build a wonderful new palace for your daughter."

"You're right," said the Sultan, who was a simple man at heart and always thought that his chief courtier knew best. He told Aladdin that he could definitely marry his daughter if he built her a marvellous palace to live in. Aladdin summoned the Genie once again, and once again the Genie did his magic.

Shortly after, a brand new palace appeared right next door to where the Sultan lived. It was the finest palace anybody had ever seen. The walls were covered with gold and silver and every room was filled with fabulous treasures. Aladdin and the Princess had a huge wedding and lived a long and happy life. Aladdin never forgot the secret of his happiness and made sure to keep his lamp safe for the rest of his days.

The Emperor's New Clothes

any years ago, there lived an Emperor. He was a very nice Emperor and kind to lots of people, but he secretly believed that no one really respected him. He thought he was a, bald, fat, silly little man who wasn't grand and important at all.

However much his wife tried to tell him everyone admired him, he refused to believe it. To try to make himself look as important as possible, he started to spend a lot of time choosing exactly the right clothes to wear. He always hired the best tailors, and made sure they used only the finest material.

The Emperor's passion for clothes grew and grew, and became widely known throughout his Empire. He had a huge room in his palace containing rows of beautiful gowns. Another room was stuffed full of different uniforms, and a third room had rolls and rolls of the most exquisite cloth piled high to the ceiling.

When he got out of bed, he would put on a magnificent silk dressing gown. After bathing, he would change into one of his many attractive robes for eating breakfast. After breakfast, he would change into something formal to discuss important matters with his ministers. Then he would change into something less formal in which to have lunch. On and on it went until, by the time he went to bed again, he'd changed his clothes more times in a day than most people would in a week!

One day, a clever swindler, pretending to be a tailor, came to see the Emperor.

"Your Majesty," began the swindler. "If you allow me to, I can make you the finest set of clothes ever seen."

These words immediately held the Emperor's interest.

"The finest clothes ever seen!" he exclaimed, excitedly.

"Yes, your Majesty," said the swindler. "In fact, these clothes are so special, they are invisible to anyone who is a complete and utter fool. Look, let me show you the cloth I'm going to use."

The swindler took precisely nothing out of his case and proceeded to show it to the Emperor.

"See how fine it is," enthused the swindler.

Not wanting to seem a complete and utter fool, the Emperor had to agree that the cloth did, indeed, look wonderful.

The Emperor told the swindler to start making his new clothes straight away, because he wanted to wear them at the next month's royal procession. The swindler was given a room of his own in the palace where he could get on with his work. Whenever anyone passed by, they could always hear through the closed door the furious whirring of his sewing machine.

After two weeks, the Emperor ordered his Prime Minister to see how his new clothes were coming along.

The Prime Minister knocked on the swindler's door.

"May I come in?" he asked. "His Excellency wishes to know how you're getting on with his new clothes."

"Of course, sir," said the swindler, opening the door.

"There's still a lot of work to do, sir," said the swindler. "But I think you'll agree that the Emperor will not be disappointed."

And, with a great flourish, he draped the new clothes along his arm for the Prime Minister to admire.

"Oh, yes. They look … well … absolutely wonderful!" said the Prime Minister, too embarrassed to say that he was looking at precisely nothing!

There was great excitement in the palace on the day of the procession. The Emperor couldn't wait to get into his new outfit, and paced nervously up and down his dressing room.

"I hope the people like me in my new clothes," he thought. "And I hope they make me look as strong and important as an Emperor should look."

When they finally arrived, the Emperor took his dressing gown off, put the new clothes on and paraded up and down in them.

"Magnificent!" exclaimed the swindler.

"You look so dignified!" gasped the Prime Minister.

"Yes, I do, don't I?" said the Emperor, rather grandly, prancing up and down in front of the mirror. "Today," he announced nobly, "I shall look like a real Emperor!"

Many people had crowded the streets in order to get a good look at the Emperor in his magnificent new clothes.

"Here he comes!" one of them yelled, spotting the Emperor stepping out of the palace.

"Doesn't he look wonderful!" exclaimed everyone, also not wishing to look foolish.

The men in the crowd bowed, and the women curtsied deeply as the Emperor passed by.

"I feel so powerful in my new clothes!" thought the Emperor, parading through the streets with his head held high.

Suddenly, a little boy stepped out from the crowd, pointed at the Emperor, and shouted:

"Wait a minute … he hasn't got any clothes on!"

There was a huge gasp from the crowd, then everyone fell silent. All of a sudden, someone tittered, another giggled, and soon everyone was laughing hysterically at their Emperor who stood before them as naked as the day he was born.

The poor Emperor had never been so humiliated in his life. He turned the brightest red, and wished the ground would open up and swallow him. Then an unusual thing happened. Instead of running away in embarrassment, he lifted his chin and began to walk grandly through the streets again. From somewhere deep inside him, the Emperor had found the courage that he'd always felt he'd lacked.

"Look at that!" said the crowd. "As naked as a newborn baby, but walking through our streets like a lion! What a man! Long Live the Emperor!"

After the procession, the Emperor rushed back to his palace. He realized he didn't need fine garments to make him feel grand and important anymore, so he gave away most of his beautiful clothes. At long last, he felt grand and important within himself. Which is just how an Emperor should feel.

The Selfish Giant

Once upon a time there was a giant who came down into the valley from his home in the mountains and built himself a castle with a beautiful garden. The giant was very proud of his new garden and all the lovely things in it. He especially liked spring, when all the pretty new flowers came out, the shrubs blossomed and a warm breeze blew through the branches in his many trees, softly rattling the leaves.

On spring days such as this, the giant liked nothing better than to open his window and hear the sound of the local children playing in his garden. They came very early in the morning, and played there the whole day until it was getting dark and time to go home.
"See you tomorrow," they waved to the giant, who gave his funny, toothless grin and waved slowly back.

One year, the giant decided to return to the mountains to visit his only friend, Horace. Horace was a giant too, and lived so high up in the mountains, it was completely barren and nearly always cold. While he was there, Horace told the gentle giant that he was foolish to let all the children play in his garden.
"I know you," said Horace, taking a big mouthful of apple pie. "You're too soft with those children. You'll let them run around until they have trampled all of your flowers! You mark my words, if you let them play in there all of the time, they will ruin your precious garden!"

The giant thought long and hard about this and came to the conclusion that Horace was right. From that moment on, his heart began to harden. "Those children don't care anything at all for my garden," he thought. "They're just using it to have fun in. Once they've ruined it, they'll just go and find somewhere else to play!"

This thought made him feel very angry. The very next day, he packed his things, said goodbye to Horace and, with his huge strides, walked back down the mountain to his castle.

Once he arrived, he opened his gate and saw all the children enjoying themselves as usual.

"Get out of my garden!" he yelled at them in his big, booming voice. "Go on, get out! You're not welcome here anymore!"

The children were very frightened. They had never seen the giant angry before, and they ran away as quickly as they could. As soon as they were gone, the giant began to build a huge wall around his garden so no one could get in. When the wall was finished, he made a sign and nailed it to the garden gate. The sign read: Private Property! Keep Out! Then he took a key out of his pocket and locked the gate.

"That's that," he said, with a satisfied look on his face, and took himself off to bed.

The next day, it started to get much colder. Winter had arrived, and with it the hail, ice and snow. But when spring came around again, and the birds began to sing and the flowers started to bloom, it was still winter inside the giant's garden. When the giant looked out of his window, he couldn't understand why winter had stayed. He missed seeing the lovely flowers and hearing the birds who nested in his trees, and he became very sad.

Years passed, and the seasons came and went, but nothing changed inside the giant's garden. It was cold and bleak, and nothing would grow. Once, when a small flower peeked its head above the ground, it quickly went back down again when it saw that the giant's garden was so unwelcoming.

One day, some children were passing by and wondered what lay behind the huge wall. They made a small hole and crawled through the wall into the garden. Each child climbed a tree, laughing and joking as they went higher and higher. When the giant pulled back his curtains, a big grin spread across his face. His garden was beautiful again! All the flowers were out, the grass was green and luscious, the bees were busy buzzing but, best of all, he heard the laughter of excited children high up in the trees, throwing blossom over themselves.

"Spring has finally returned!" he cried, and rushed outside.

But in the farthest corner of the garden, the giant saw a sad sight. A

little boy was crying because he wasn't tall enough to climb a tree. Seeing the boy so upset, melted the giant's heart. He reached down, picked the boy up and gently sat him in the branches of a tree.

"I've been so selfish, not allowing the children to play in my garden," he thought. "No wonder winter wanted to stay."

But when the other children saw him, they became scared and started to run away.

"Don't go," pleaded the giant. "This is your garden now. Look!"

Then he fetched the biggest axe he could find and knocked down the wall down until it was nothing but dust.

When the people of the town passed by, they couldn't believe what they

saw. The giant was enjoying himself! He was lying in the middle of the garden, laughing uncontrollably as the children clambered and played all over him.

From that day on, the children came to play in the giant's garden whenever they could. Often, the giant would play with them and, in the warm evenings, tell them stories of his ancestors who had never been out of the mountains.

As the giant got older, it became more difficult for him to move around,

so he liked to sit in his big armchair by the window, watching the children playing in the garden.

"What a stupid giant I was before," he'd think, "building a wall that kept me away from all this happiness. Thank goodness I realized my mistake."

Then he'd shut his eyes and, with the sound of children's laughter ringing in his ears, he'd fall into a long, contented sleep.